NAILED IT!

Extreme
MotoGP

Virginia Loh-Hagan

45th Parallel Press

Published in the United States of America by Cherry Lake Publishing
Ann Arbor, Michigan
www.cherrylakepublishing.com

Content Adviser: Liv Williams, Editor, www.iLivExtreme.com
Reading Adviser: Marla Conn, ReadAbility, Inc.
Photo Credits: ©Zryzner/Shutterstock.com, 5; ©Gold & Goose/Red Bull Content Pool, 6; ©Natursports/Shutterstock.com, 8; ©Rainer Herhaus/Shutterstock.com, 11; ©Gold & Goose/Red Bull Content Pool, 13; ©Gold & Goose/Red Bull Content Pool, 15; ©Gold & Goose/Red Bull Content Pool, 17; ©Red Bull Media House/Red Bull Content Pool, 19; ©Tom Morgan/Alamy Stock Photo, 21; ©Gold & Goose/Red Bull Content Pool, 22; ©GEPA pictures/Red Bull Content Pool, 25; ©Christian Pondella/Red Bull Content Pool, 27; ©Gold & Goose/Red Bull Content Pool, 29; ©Trusjom/Shutterstock.com, multiple interior pages; ©Kues/Shutterstock.com, multiple interior pages

Copyright © 2017 by Cherry Lake Publishing
All rights reserved. No part of this book may be reproduced or utilized in any form or by any means without written permission from the publisher.

45th Parallel Press is an imprint of Cherry Lake Publishing.

Library of Congress Cataloging-in-Publication Data

Names: Loh-Hagan, Virginia.
Title: Extreme MotoGP / by Virginia Loh-Hagan.
Description: Ann Arbor : Cherry Lake Publishing, [2016] | Series: Nailed it!
 | Includes bibliographical references and index.
Identifiers: LCCN 2015049731| ISBN 9781634710916 (hardcover) | ISBN
 9781634711906 (pdf) | ISBN 9781634712897 (paperback) | ISBN 9781634713887
 (ebook)
Subjects: LCSH: Grand Prix motorcycle racing--Juvenile literature. | Extreme
 sports--Juvenile literature.
Classification: LCC GV1060 .L65 2016 | DDC 796.7/5--dc23
LC record available at http://lccn.loc.gov/2015049731

Printed in the United States of America
Corporate Graphics Inc.

ABOUT THE AUTHOR

Dr. Virginia Loh-Hagan is an author, university professor, former classroom teacher, and curriculum designer. She went on a motorcycle ride, once. She lives in San Diego with her very tall husband and very naughty dogs. To learn more about her, visit www.virginialoh.com.

Table of Contents

About the Author 2

CHAPTER 1:
Superstars of MotoGP 4

CHAPTER 2:
Racing and Winning 10

CHAPTER 3:
MotoGP Equipment 16

CHAPTER 4:
History of MotoGP 20

CHAPTER 5:
Racing Dangers 24

Did You Know? 30

Consider This! 31

Learn More 31

Glossary 32

Index 32

Superstars of MotoGP

Who are the superstars of MotoGP? Why are they special?

Marc Márquez rides fast. He's perched on top of his bike. His muscles tense. He adjusts his speed. He twitches his upper body. He balances. He leans in. He tilts his bike. He takes sharp corners. He's close to the ground. He scrapes his elbows. He scrapes his shoulders.

He's in the **pole position**. He's doing well. He's in the first row. He's in the inside lane. He was overtaken by a champion rider. But he still has 21 more laps to go. He rides smart. He became the youngest rider to win a MotoGP race. He won more races. He became the world's youngest MotoGP champion!

Valentino Rossi has won many world championships. He was racing. He was fighting for third place. He put pressure on another rider. He ran off track. He ran downhill. His bike's rear wheel slid. He got kicked off his bike. A wheel hit him. He got knocked out. He tumbled. He crashed. He was taken to the hospital. He injured his brain. He broke a finger.

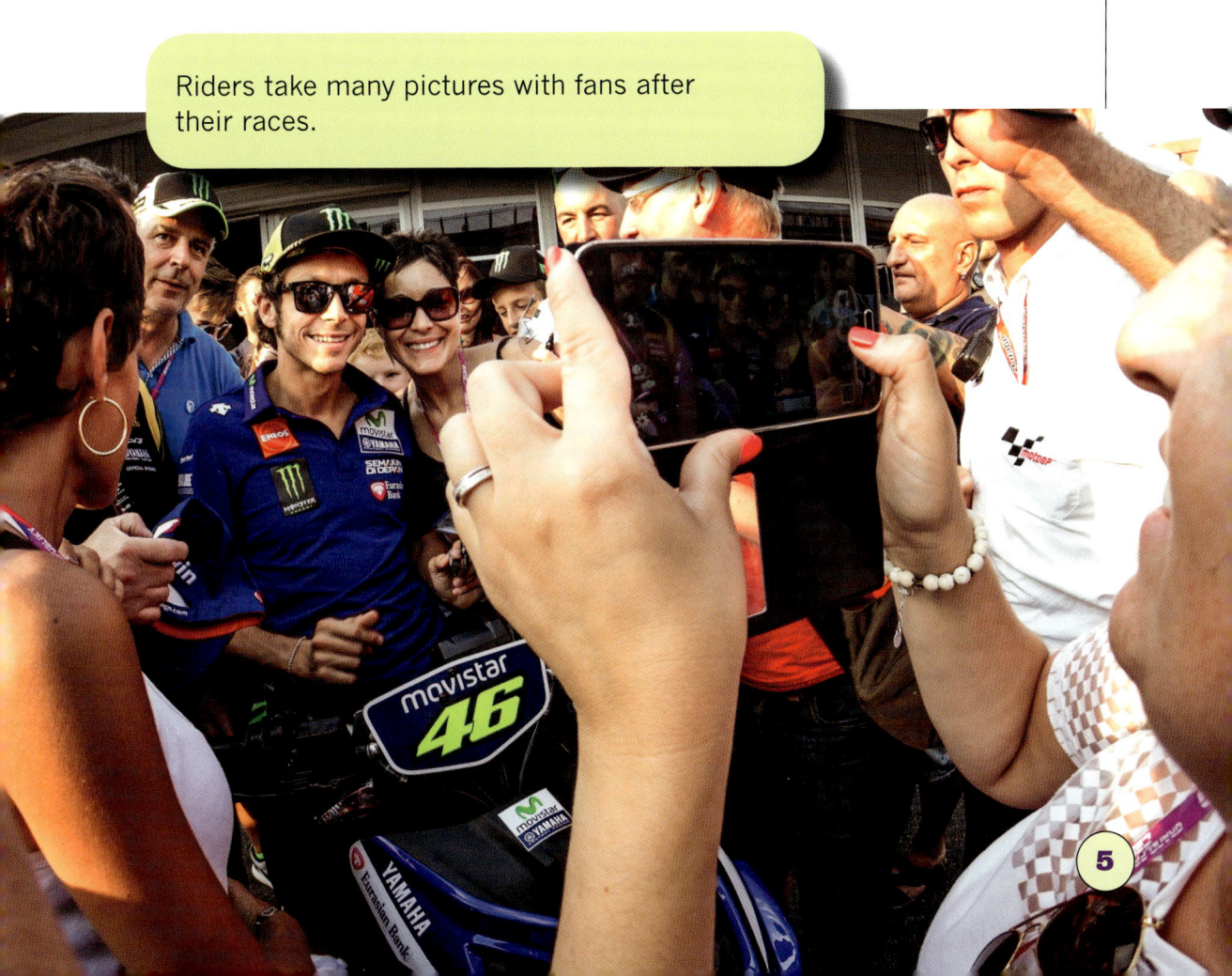

Riders take many pictures with fans after their races.

Riders change their riding styles to match their daredevil competitors.

Rossi loves MotoGP. He has had many injuries. He's had broken legs. He refused to quit. He exercised in pools. He trained. He recovered.

He's one of the oldest riders. But he won't let age stop him either.

Cameron Beaubier is a motorcycle racer. He's breaking into MotoGP. He's from the United States. There aren't many American riders. He's riding. He's racing. He's competing.

He relies on his speed. But he needed more. He needed structure. He needed guidance.

NAILED IT!

Spotlight Biography: Ana Carrasco Gabarrón

Ana Carrasco Gabarrón is from Spain. She got her first bike at age 3. She started racing at age 4. She said, "I just rode the bike because I liked it. But now in the world championships, things are more serious." She is a MotoGP racer. She competes in world championships. She started competing at age 16. She was the first female to score points. After that race she said, "I think I had a very good race and I am very pleased. I struggled a bit at the start." She had a hard time getting positions in the race. She had six laps to go. She got to the front of her group. She passed others at the end of the final lap. She got her first world championship point. She said, "I'm super happy!"

HJC
YAMAHA
PETRONAS
YAMALUBE
SEMAKIN DI DEPAN
11
WITH YOU JAPAN
PETRONAS
YAMAHA
SEMAKIN DI DEPAN

Ben Spies is coaching him. Beaubier said, "Ben was our last American world champion … Ben has a ton of experience traveling in Europe. And it's no secret that's where I want to be in the future."

Spies knows racetracks. He can teach Beaubier about riding. He can teach him about training. Beaubier is smart. He learns from the best.

Racing and Winning

What is MotoGP? What is some basic information about MotoGP racing? How do riders prepare for MotoGP racing?

MotoGP stands for motorcycle **grand prix**. Grand prix means a great prize. The MotoGP World Championship is the top contest for motorcycle road racing.

There are three types of motorcycle racing. Moto2 and Moto3 are lower levels of racing. MotoGP is the top level. It's the hardest level. It has the biggest engines. It has the highest speeds.

MotoGP riders race at top speeds. They race at 215 miles (346 kilometers) per hour. They twist. They turn. They corner at 110 miles (177 km) per hour. They lean close to the ground.

The MotoGP riders work 9 months of the year. The racing season is from March to November. They travel 180 days a year. They travel all around the world.

Races take place on race **circuits**. Circuits are racetracks. They're at least 59 miles (95 km) long. They're no longer than 80 miles (128.7 km). Races last 45 minutes.

The MotoGP championship has 18 races. It takes place in 14 countries. Each race lasts 3 days. There are 2 days of practice and **qualifying**. Qualifying means trying out to compete. The last day is the races.

MotoGP has been called Formula 1 racing on two wheels.

Riders get points. They get points for their positions. The most points wins. The top three winners earn a **podium** spot. A podium is a tall stand.

> **NAILED IT!**
>
> ## Advice from the Field: Jorge Lorenzo
>
> Jorge Lorenzo is from Spain. He's a MotoGP world champion. He likes competing. He advises riders to learn from their mistakes. He said, "I would say that in racing every experience has its value. …You have to be patient and be motivated to keep working and training to overcome the bad times." He likes winning. He said, "We must get more points than the others. And that's achieved with a great bike, staying focused, being one of the fastest and not failing." He advises being a lifelong learner. He said, "I hope to always keep an open mind so I can learn from everything and everyone around me. And I'm able to enjoy the process of learning and growing in life. We must learn. But also live in the moment and enjoy it."

Races are held in Italy, Spain, Japan, the United States, and other countries.

MotoGP riders stay in race positions. They do this for 45 minutes. They use their bodies. They brake. They drive. They balance. They lean. They're intense. MotoGP is hard on bodies.

Riders have to be physically fit. They prepare their bodies for the strain of riding. So, they run. They cycle. They cross-train. They ride road bikes. They ride motocross bikes.

They ride trial bikes.

Jorge Lorenzo trains in many different ways. He said, "When you get on the MotoGP bike the first day, you have aches all throughout your body. The physical exertion you get from riding a MotoGP bike is different from everything else. But training does help."

A lean angle is the degree at which riders tilt their bikes into the track as they take corners at high speeds.

3

MotoGP Equipment

What is a MotoGP bike like? What does a MotoGP rider need?

MotoGP riders depend on their motorcycles. These are special bikes. They're racing machines. They can't be ridden on public roads. Regular people can't buy them.

Each engine is individually made. They're made of light, strong material. But they're still heavy. They weigh about 330 pounds (149.7 kg). They reach speeds of 220 miles (354 km) per hour.

MotoGP bikes have a lot of technology. They have 30 to 40 **sensors**. Sensors pick up information. A computer keeps track of everything. Riders look at **gears**. Gears control speeds. They control power. Riders look at lap times.

These bikes work in extreme conditions. So, their parts don't last long.

MotoGP riders need **leathers**. Leathers are the riders' suits. They're made of leather. They protect riders during high-speed crashes. They have extra padding in the elbows, shoulders, and knees. They feel like a second skin. This is so riders can move around easily.

It's illegal to ride MotoGP bikes on regular roads.

Extreme MotoGP: Know the Lingo

Apex: the tightest point on a corner

Braking marker: a point a rider uses to judge braking

Endo: stopping a bike to lift the rear wheel off the ground

Hairpin: a very tight corner that has to be taken slowly

High side: a crash in which the rear wheel of the bike slides out from under the rider

Hole-shot: leading the race at the first corner

Low side: a crash in which the rear wheel or both wheels lose control, causing the bike to slip out from underneath the rider

Pit-box: a temporary garage

Slicks: tires with no tread

Tire wall: stacked tires used as a crash barrier to reduce damage and injury on impact

Topping the timesheet: recording the fastest time

Wheelie: lifting the front wheel of a bike

Leathers are made for crashing and sliding.

Some leathers have an airbag. The airbag protects the rider's upper body.

Riders wear other protective gear. They wear a helmet. The helmet covers the entire face. They wear racing boots. They wear racing gloves.

4

History of MotoGP

How did MotoGP develop? Who were the main heroes in MotoGP history?

The first motorcycle was sold in 1894. It was made in Germany. The first race took place in France. In 1907, Britain hosted the Tourist Trophy. This race took place on the Isle of Man. Motorsports became popular in Europe.

World War II affected the races. Gas was not available. Then, the war ended. Races started happening again. A **federation** was formed. This is an official group. It created rules. It organized the MotoGP competition. The first one was in 1949. MotoGP is the world's oldest motorsports championship.

Italians dominated the races. They won races. They made bikes. That changed in the 1960s. The Japanese made bikes. Their bikes are still used today. Kunimitsu Takahashi was the first Japanese winner.

FIM stands for the Fédération Internationale de Motocyclisme.

Bike companies also competed against each other. Each wanted to be the best bike company!

Giacomo Agostini became famous in the 1960s. He's the greatest motorcycle racer. He has won 122 Grand Prix wins. He's won 15 world championships. He retired in 1977. But he became a coach. He mentored MotoGP riders.

There were many **rivals** in the 1980s. Rivals are people competing against each other. This made races more exciting. Kenny Roberts and Freddie Spencer were popular rivals. They were equal. They constantly fought. They wanted to be the best.

Technology got better. Bikes improved each year. Engines got more powerful. Bikes became slimmer. This allowed for higher speeds.

NAILED IT!

That Happened?!?

Nothing stops MotoGP riders. Except for a runaway dog! MotoGP Red Bull Grand Prix of The Americas is a competition. Riders were practicing. But they had to stop. A 1-year-old dog appeared on the track. The dog was a Shiba Inu mix. The dog got in front of Maverick Viñales. Viñales is a rider. Grand Prix of the Americas tweeted, "Slight delay as a stray dog has found its way on track. Animal Control is en route to deal with the situation." The practice session was red-flagged. Red-flag means stop. The race was delayed 15 minutes. Officials rounded up the dog. No riders hit it. A week later, the dog was adopted. The dog's name is Moto.

Racing Dangers

What are some dangers of MotoGP? Who are some riders who have suffered doing MotoGP?

Casey Stoner was in the lead. He entered a corner. He was at high speed. A part of his bike got stuck. He missed the turn. He shot off the track. His bike flipped. He spun through the air. His bike got wrecked. He crawled on all fours. He crawled to safety. He went to the hospital. He broke his leg. He broke his shoulder. His leathers, boots, and helmet saved him. He said, "I would have been much worse off without them."

Alex de Angelis was practicing. He crashed. His brain was bleeding. He broke his back. He broke two ribs. He broke his chest. He hurt his neck. He damaged his lungs.

Marco Simoncelli was special. He had big hair. He was over 6 feet (1.8 meters) tall. Fans loved him. He was in a race. He turned a corner. He lost control. His bike slid. He crashed into other riders. He lost his helmet. He was hit. He had many injuries. He died.

Scott Redding is a MotoGP racer. He's lost many friends. He said, "This is not racing anymore. It's like a death race." He said riders are glad to be alive. He thinks the bikes are too advanced.

Danger is part of the job. Safety standards are important to follow.

MotoGP riders risk their lives. They ride at high speeds. They ride powerful machines. They could get hurt. They could die.

NAILED IT!

When Extreme Is Too Extreme!

Motovelocidad del Valle is a road race. It takes place in Colombia. Regular people created the event. It's more dangerous than MotoGP. These riders don't go as fast. But the road is scarier. The road has many obstacles, or objects. Riders have to learn the track. There aren't any signs. Curbs, houses, light posts, and people are all over. The ground is not smooth. For safety, mattresses are tied to trees. Tires are stacked around corners. There aren't any run-off areas. Crashing is dangerous to both riders and spectators. Spectators are audience members. A rider crashed. He was thrown to the ground. He hit the middle of the road. The first five riders swerved past the fallen rider. But other riders crashed. They suffered major injuries.

27

MotoGP is dangerous. It's even more dangerous in bad weather. Riders study their tracks. They rely on certain things. Any changes can throw off a race.

There was a race in Italy. The rain came down. There were 62 crashes. The main cause was the wet track. The track became slick. Riders had less grip on the track. It wasn't safe to brake while racing. Riders glided.

Riders bring extra tires. There are special tires for rain. Some riders prefer wet races. They use it as a chance to get ahead.

MotoGP riders live life in the fast lane!

Wet races are races in the rain. Dry races are races in sunny weather.

Did You Know?

- Riders lose about 9 cups (2.1 liters) of sweat during a race.

- Tires cost about $1,200 per pair.

- Some riders wear kangaroo leather. It's the most flexible leather.

- Some riders crash. They will still be included in the results table if they complete 75 percent of the race.

- There are over 10 different flags used in MotoGP. The flags are used to signal the riders.

- Riders can finish the race and get points even if their bikes are broken. They need to be in contact with the bikes. They can even get help from their teams.

- Tires get hot. They can reach 250 degrees Fahrenheit (121 degrees Celsius).

- The Indianapolis Motor Speedway oval covers 253 acres (102 hectares). It's the world's largest spectator sporting facility. It has over 250,000 seats.

- There are about 11 timekeepers in one race. They work on official race times. Five people record times. The others double-check times.

- The Tomahawk is the world's fastest superbike. Its top speed is over 400 miles (643.7 km) per hour. Only 10 were built. It costs $550,000.

Consider This!

TAKE A POSITION! Some people think motorcycle racing is not a sport. They think motorcycles do all the work. Do you think MotoGP is a sport or not? Argue your point with reasons and evidence.

SAY WHAT? Learn more about all three classes of motorcycle racing. Explain how they are different. Explain how they are similar. Explain how and why MotoGP is the most extreme of all three classes.

THINK ABOUT IT! Famous rivals helped promote the sport of MotoGP. Think of movies, books, or history. What are some other famous rivals? How is having rivals positive? How is having rivals negative?

SEE A DIFFERENT SIDE! Reread Chapter 5. Why do you think parents wouldn't want their children competing in MotoGP races? What are some rules you would create to make MotoGP safer?

Learn More: Resources

PRIMARY SOURCES

Fastest, a documentary (2011, Media X International).

Hitting the Apex, a documentary (2015, Universal Pictures), http://hittingtheapexfilm.com.

SECONDARY SOURCES

David, Jack. *Sport Bikes*. Minneapolis: Bellwether Media, 2008.

Scott, Michael. *Moto GP: Yesterday & Today*. London: Carlton Books, 2014.

Zuehlke, Jeffrey. *Motorcycle Road Racing*. Minneapolis: Lerner Publications, 2009.

WEB SITES

Fédération Internationale de Motocyclisme: www.fim-live.com

Motorcycle Roadracing Association: www.mra-racing.org

Red Bull MotoGP: http://www.redbull.com/us/en/motorsports/motogp

Glossary

circuits (SUR-kits) oval racetracks; racing laps

federation (fed-uh-RAY-shuhn) official organization that establishes rules and guidelines

gears (GEERZ) machine parts that control speed on bikes

grand prix (GRAND PREE) great prize, a grand racing event

leathers (LETH-urz) racing suits that provide protection to the riders

podium (POH-dee-uhm) a tall stand for the top three winners

pole position (POHL puh-ZISH-uhn) spot in the inside lane of the front row

qualifying (KWAH-luh-fye-ing) tryout races that decide who can compete in the final race

rivals (RYE-vuhlz) competing opponents

sensors (SEN-surz) things that pick up information

Index

circuits, 11
competitions, 7, 10
crashes, 5, 17, 24, 25, 26, 28

dangers, 24–27
deaths, 25

equipment, 16–19

injuries, 5, 6, 24–25, 26

leathers, 17, 19, 28
lingo, 18

MotoGP
  dangers, 24–27
  equipment, 16–19
  famous drivers, 4–9, 12, 22–23
  history of, 20–23
  training for, 13–14
  what it is, 10–15

motorcycles, 10, 16–17, 20–21

protective gear, 19

rain, 27

tires, 27, 28